HELLO!
57

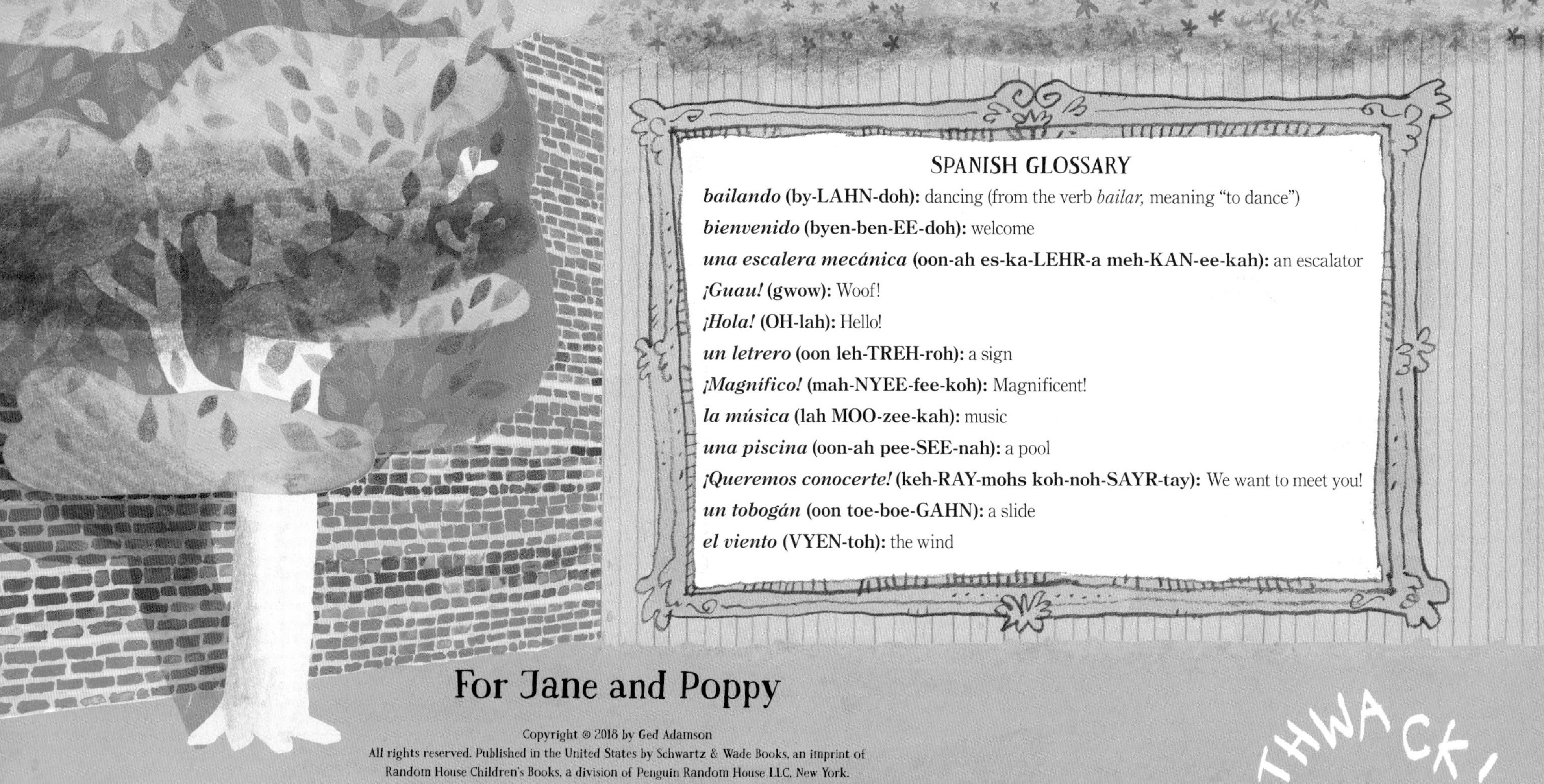

SPANISH GLOSSARY

***bailando* (by-LAHN-doh):** dancing (from the verb *bailar,* meaning "to dance")

***bienvenido* (byen-ben-EE-doh):** welcome

***una escalera mecánica* (oon-ah es-ka-LEHR-a meh-KAN-ee-kah):** an escalator

***¡Guau!* (gwow):** Woof!

***¡Hola!* (OH-lah):** Hello!

***un letrero* (oon leh-TREH-roh):** a sign

***¡Magnífico!* (mah-NYEE-fee-koh):** Magnificent!

***la música* (lah MOO-zee-kah):** music

***una piscina* (oon-ah pee-SEE-nah):** a pool

***¡Queremos conocerte!* (keh-RAY-mohs koh-noh-SAYR-tay):** We want to meet you!

***un tobogán* (oon toe-boe-GAHN):** a slide

***el viento* (VYEN-toh):** the wind

For Jane and Poppy

 Published in the United States by Schwartz & Wade Books, an imprint of Random House Children's Books, a division of Penguin Random House LLC, New York.
Schwartz & Wade Books and the colophon are trademarks of Penguin Random House LLC.
Visit us on the Web! rhcbooks.com
Educators and librarians, for a variety of teaching tools, visit us at RHTeachersLibrarians.com
Library of Congress Cataloging-in-Publication Data
Names: Adamson, Ged, author.
Title: Douglas, you're a genius! / by Ged Adamson.
Other titles: Douglas, you are a genius!
Description: First edition. | New York : Schwartz & Wade, [2018] | Summary: Nancy and Douglas, determined to learn what is on the other side of a fence, try Nancy's plans to launch, vault, and fly Douglas over, then succeed with Douglas's simple idea.
Identifiers: LCCN 2017045773 (print) | LCCN 2017057187 (ebook) | ISBN 978-1-5247-6532-3 (ebook)
ISBN 978-1-5247-6530-9 (hardcover) | ISBN 978-1-5247-6531-6 (library binding)
Subjects: | CYAC: Fences—Fiction. | Lost and found possessions—Fiction. | Dogs—Fiction.
Classification: LCC PZ7.A2315 (ebook) | LCC PZ7.A2315 Dr 2018 (print) | DDC [E]—dc23

The text of this book is set in Mrs. Ant.
The illustrations were rendered in pencil and watercolor.

MANUFACTURED IN CHINA
2 4 6 8 10 9 7 5 3 1
First Edition

by Ged Adamson

schwartz & wade books • new york

Nancy and Douglas were playing ball in the backyard, when Nancy hit one too hard.

"Oops!" cried Nancy. "There it goes."

Then something mysterious happened.

Nancy and
Douglas called
into the hole.

But there was
no response.

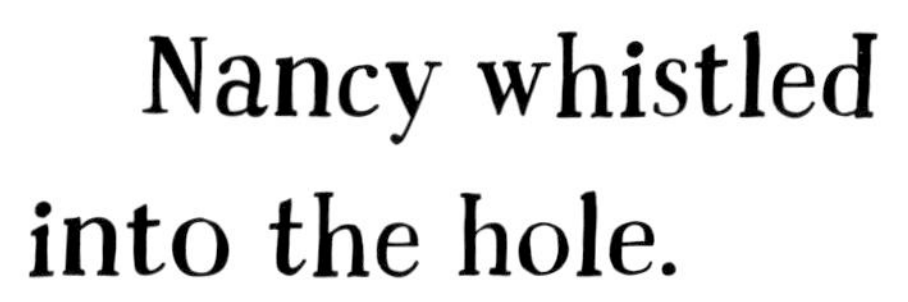

Nancy whistled
into the hole.

Douglas barked
into the hole.

But still nothing.

Who's over there? Douglas wondered. He had an idea how to find out.

Nancy and Douglas hoped it would work.

They waited.

And waited.

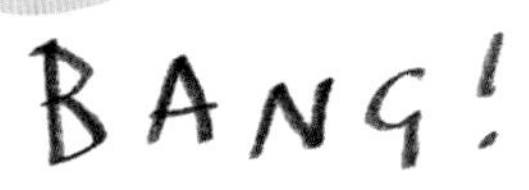

And waited.

And waited some more, until . . .

Nancy tried to sound out the words, but she had no idea what they meant.

"I don't know what they mean either, but now I really want to see who's on the other side of this fence!"

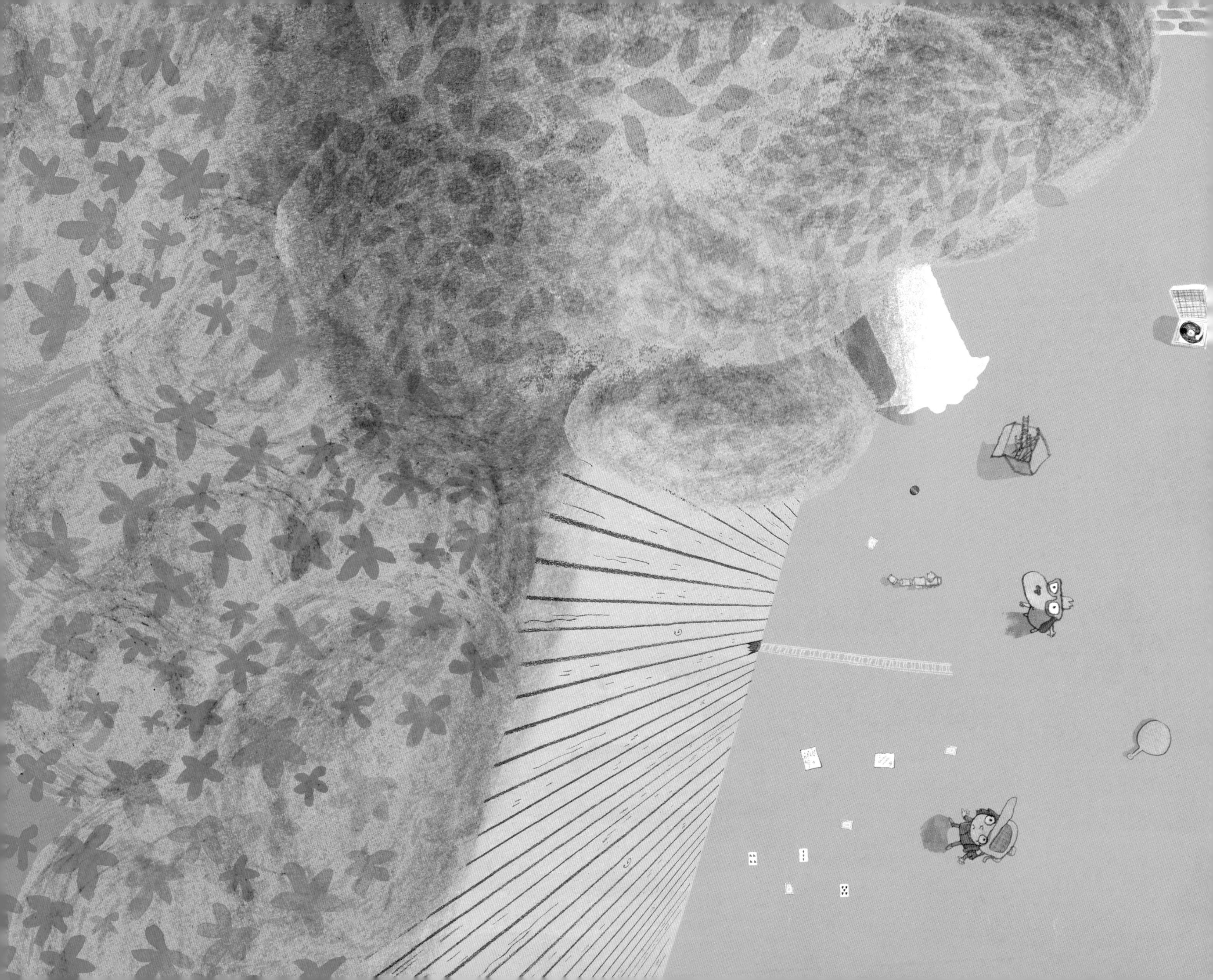

They looked side to side. They looked up.
“It’s kind of high,” said Douglas.
“Have no fear—I have a plan!” Nancy cried.

"What do you think?" Nancy asked.

"I think it looks dangerous," muttered Douglas.

RUBBER BANDS
"Nonsense," said Nancy.
"You'll be fine!
Just run,
jump,
and bounce!"
"Waaaaaahhhhhh!"

"Almost!" Nancy exclaimed. "You really got some nice elevation!"

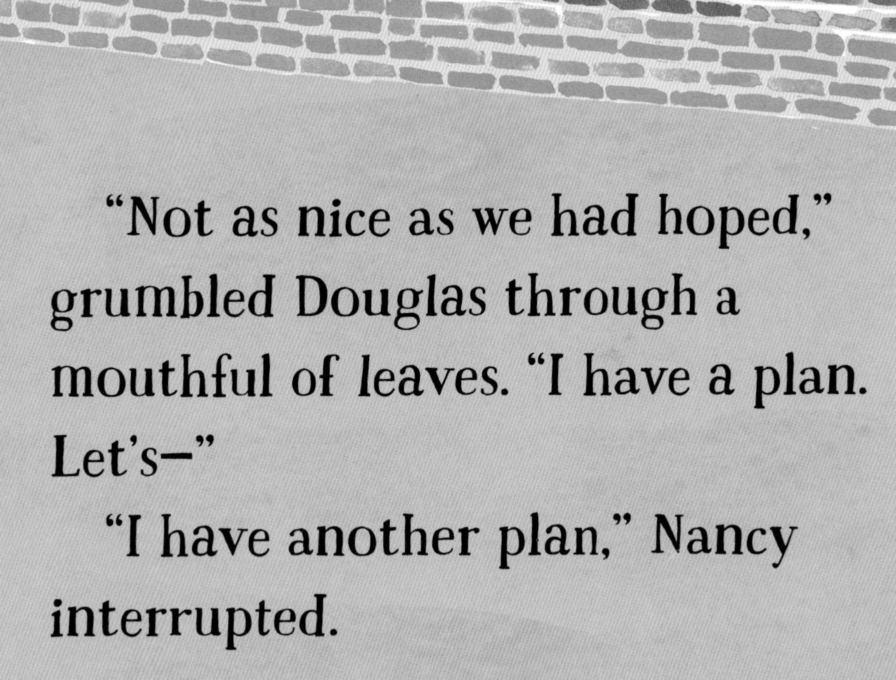

“Not as nice as we had hoped,” grumbled Douglas through a mouthful of leaves. “I have a plan. Let’s—”

“I have another plan,” Nancy interrupted.

"I'm not sure about this," Douglas groaned.

"Where's your sense of adventure, Douglas?" asked Nancy. And before he could say another word, she yanked the strings.

Douglas moved astonishingly fast, but unfortunately, not in an upward direction.

"Can we please try my plan now?" he asked.
But Nancy wasn't finished yet.

She had lots of ideas, and Douglas tried them all.

But finally Douglas had had enough.

"Fine, but I can already tell that this is a silly idea," Nancy said.

Douglas started digging.

And digging some more.

Finally, he stopped.
"I knew you'd give up," said Nancy.

"I didn't give up. I'm finished," said Douglas. "Look behind you."

“Douglas, you’re a genius!”

Don't look down, Nancy!

By the time they reached the top, they were in for a big surprise.

Hello!
¡HOLA!
WOOF!
¡GUAU!

The new friends got busy right away on a new plan.

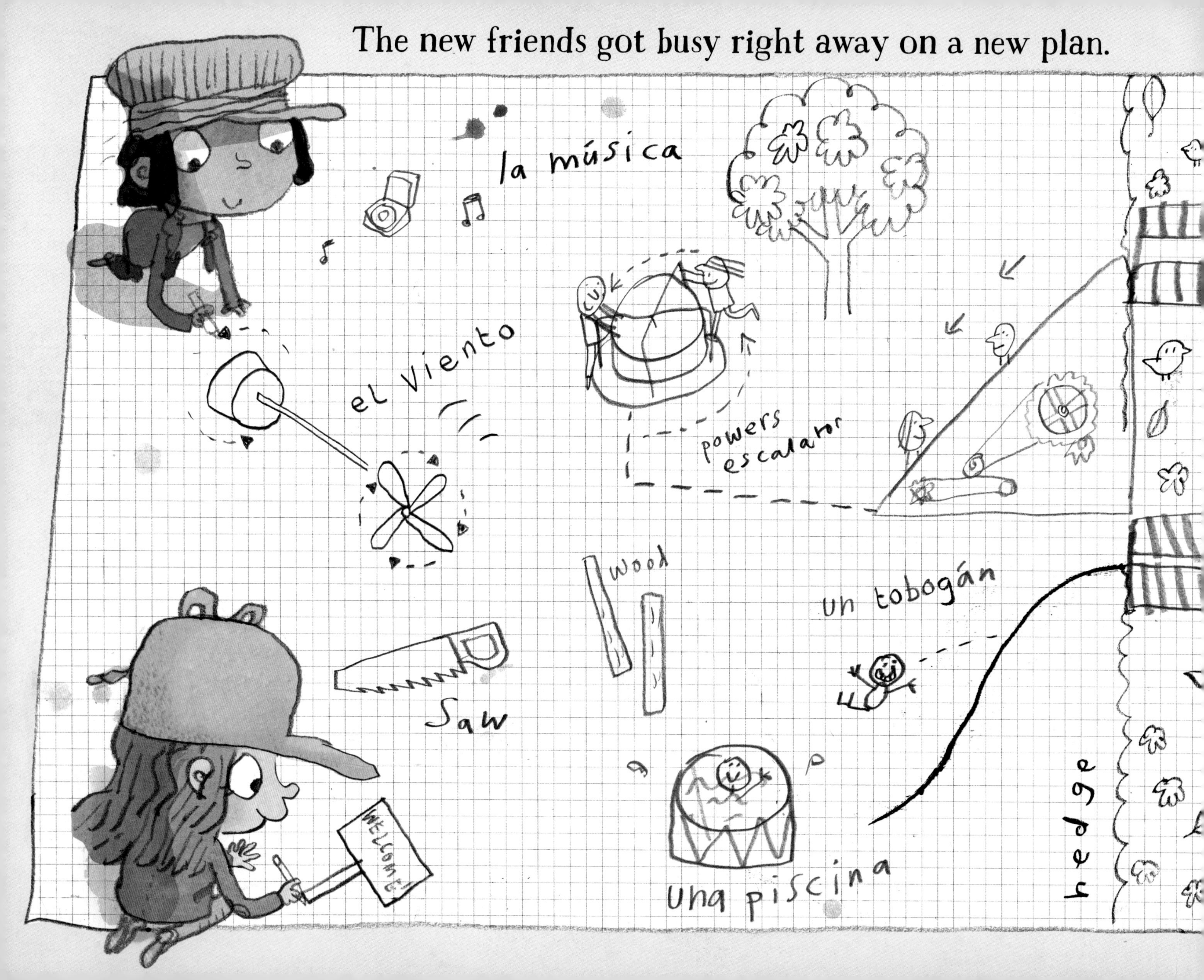

hedge
we will
need help
SLIDE!
Yay!
lots of
plastic
balls
un
Letrero
BIENVENIDO
Hammers
and
nails
connected
to
escalator!
Una escalera
mecánica
make
wheels
bailando

And it was the most genius plan of all.

Magnificent!
BIENVENIDO

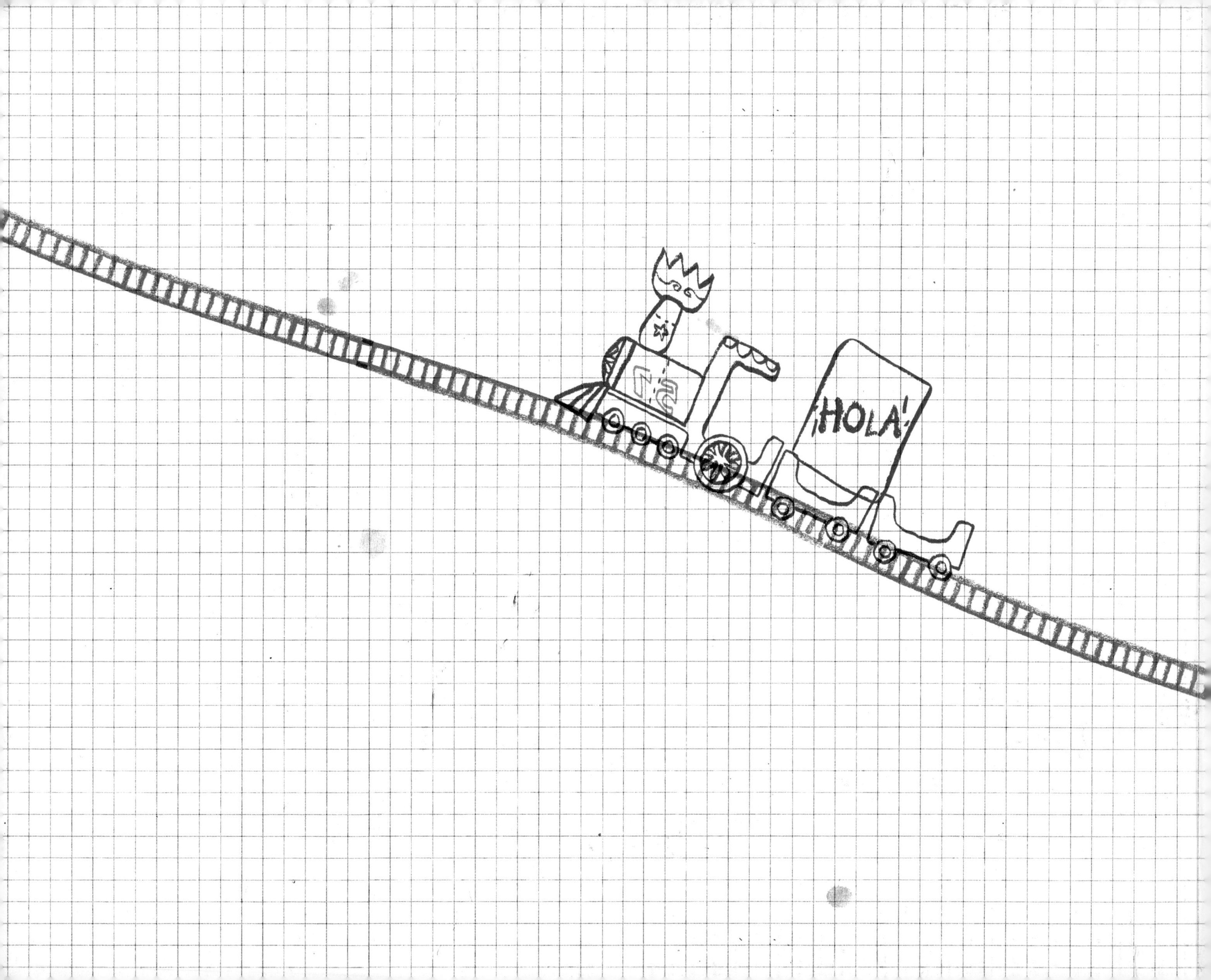
¡HOLA!